## CAPTAIN SCARLET

He's the one who knows the Mysteron game,
And things they plan.

## CAPTAIN SCARLET

To his Martian foes a dangerous name,
A superman!

They crash him, and his body they burn.
They smash him, but they know he'll return
To live again –

## CAPTAIN SCARLET

As the Angels are flying wing to wing
Into the scene,
Spectrum Is Green!

## CAPTAIN SCARLET

Though the Mysterons plan to conquer the Earth,
This indestructible man will show what he's worth.

The indestructible
CAPTAIN SCARLET!

The CAPTAIN SCARLET
AND THE MYSTERONS series,
published by Young Corgi Books:

# THE MYSTERONS

# 1

## Written by
# Dave Morris

CAPTAIN SCARLET AND THE MYSTERONS:
THE MYSTERONS
A YOUNG CORGI BOOK 0 552 52786 6

First publication in Great Britain

PRINTING HISTORY
Young Corgi edition published 1993
Reprinted 1993

CAPTAIN SCARLET AND THE MYSTERONS © ITC
ENTERTAINMENT GROUP LTD.
LICENSED BY COPYRIGHT PROMOTIONS LTD.

Set in 13½pt Linotype New Century Schoolbook by
Phoenix Typesetting, Ilkley, West Yorkshire.

Young Corgi Books are published by
Transworld Publishers Ltd,
61–63 Uxbridge Road, Ealing, London W5 5SA,
in Australia by Transworld Publishers (Australia) Pty. Ltd,
15–25 Helles Avenue, Moorebank, NSW 2170,
and in New Zealand by Transworld Publishers (N.Z.) Ltd,
3 William Pickering Drive, Albany, Auckland.

Printed and bound in Great Britain by
Cox & Wyman Ltd, Reading, Berks.

# THE MYSTERONS

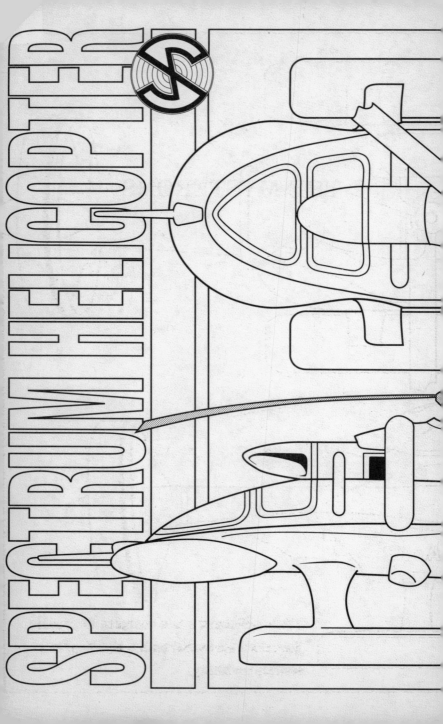

These helicopters are designed to provide
Spectrum personnel with a high degree of
manoeuverability.

# WAR IS DECLARED

Outside was a landscape of low crags and rusty brown sand. Even with the sun up, the sky was violet and a few stars were visible like gleaming pebbles. There was no scene like that anywhere on Earth. It could only be Mars.

Captain Black turned from the window. 'Let's go exploring,' he said to the astronaut sitting beside him.

The man touched a button and a ramp lowered from the side of the spaceship. Their three-man exploration buggy trundled down the ramp until Black heard its caterpillar

9

tracks crunch on the red gravel of the Martian terrain. 'Let's try over that ridge,' Black said to the driver.

Captain Black disliked missions like this. He was one of Spectrum's top agents, and had often bravely faced ruthless terrorists and spies in the course of his duty, but this was different. He knew that it would only take a small crack in the buggy's chassis for all their air to go hissing off into the thin Martian atmosphere, and then he and the others would be freeze-dried in seconds. It was the idea of dying helplessly that Black hated.

The third man in the team, the radio operator, interrupted Black's brooding thoughts. 'I've pinpointed the origin of the radio signals Spectrum picked up,' he said excitedly. 'It's just over the crest of this hill . . .'

His voice trailed off. All three men just sat and stared in amazement at what lay in front of them. Black shook his head, not sure if he was seeing

things. He had always believed that Mars was a dead world – as barren as the Moon. Everyone had believed that.

Everyone had been wrong. In the valley ahead was a city of glittering towers and domes, all bathed in the strange unearthly glow of coloured lights.

'Life on Mars!' gasped the radio operator. 'It's incredible. Just think, this will be mankind's first contact with an alien intelligence – and we haven't just got front-row tickets, we're part of the action!'

Inside the city, Martian thoughts mirrored the Earthmen's excitement. Alien instruments had tracked the progress of the spacecraft from Earth, and now an image formed on a screen that looked like a giant water-droplet. 'The first of the Earth space-travellers have arrived,' said one of the alien scientists. 'They share our curiosity about the universe. We must welcome them.'

'Let us take a closer look at our newfound allies,' suggested another of the aliens. He played a glittering light across the instrument console in front of him, and a switch dilated like the iris of an eye.

Outside, large cameras began to swivel so as to get a better view of the Earthmen's buggy. But the aliens, ignorant of the ways of warfare, had made a crucial mistake. Their cameras looked to human eyes like huge cannons. 'They're getting

ready to attack!' cried the driver of the buggy.

Fifteen years in law enforcement had taught Captain Black to respond instantly. His finger stabbed out at the button priming the buggy's missiles. It was to be the most fateful moment in all of history.

The only voice of reason was the radio operator. 'Wait,' he started to say, 'maybe they're not hostile—'

Too late. Flicking off the safety lock, Black fired the missiles. They roared through the sparse Martian atmosphere, exploding with devastating force in the bottom of the valley. The alien towers toppled and the domes caved in. Black fired another barrage, and then another, until they could see nothing but a pall of fine pink dust. As the dust settled, it was obvious

that the aliens had been taken completely unawares. Their city was now just a tangled rubble of broken metal girders and smouldering crystal.

Black narrowed his eyes, surveying the wreckage with neither pleasure nor regret. In his view, it was kill or be killed. 'Go and get our spacesuits, lieutenant,' he said to the radio operator. 'We'll need to collect some samples of the debris for the Spectrum boffins to analyse back home.'

The lieutenant was unbuckling his seatbelt when suddenly he caught sight of something moving in the ruined city. 'Look!' he said.

Up through the rubble poked a turret-like structure. The dust and rocks fell away from its domed surface as it rose higher. Then the sections of the dome opened like steel petals to reveal a curious ray-projector. The projector flared into life, sending a hard grey-white beam lancing down into the twisted wreckage of the alien city.

'They're going to retaliate!' cried the driver in panic. 'Let's get out of here—'

Captain Black caught his arm. 'No,' he said. 'We have to report this to Spectrum, if we can.' He opened a radio link, so that whatever they heard would be relayed back to Earth. Black was ice-cool now in the face of deadly danger. His earlier nervousness was gone. If he had to die at the hands of an alien enemy, at least that was what he had been trained for. And he would go down fighting.

Little did Black know that the Mysterons had a far worse fate than death in store for him.

As the beam of light bathed the wreckage, a strange thing happened. It looked like a video being played in reverse. Motes of dust swirled down out of the air. Bent girders straightened themselves, moving like metal snakes, and concrete leapt up from the ground to cover them. In less than a minute the entire city had re-formed, exactly as it was before the missiles hit.

'They can reverse time . . .' Black realized. 'Energy transformed into matter: entropy reduced to order! But . . . that would make them unbeatable.'

'And you may have just started a war with them,' said the radio operator. As an afterthought, he added ironically: 'Sir.'

Now a voice echoed from the alien city. It was a deep voice, like wind roaring inside the crater of volcano, and one which all mankind would come in time to know and dread. 'Earthmen,' it said, 'we are peaceful beings and yet you tried to destroy us. Now you know that you cannot succeed – our scientific knowledge makes us indestructible. We were willing to share this knowledge with you, but it is now clear to us that your species is too aggressive.

17

We shall retaliate for this unprovoked attack, and our retaliation will eventually mean the end of life on Earth. We do not view this as war: humanity is like a dangerous virus, and like a virus it must be eradicated. Our first act will be to assassinate your World President. This is the voice of the Mysterons. We know that you can hear us . . .'

Six weeks later, Captains Scarlet and Brown were driving through the rural landscape of upstate New York, on their way to pick up the World President. Captain Scarlet's personal radio gave a bleep, but in the world of 2068 there was no need for car phones. Instead, a small radio microphone flipped down from the peak of his cap. 'Captain Scarlet,' said the voice of Colonel White,

Spectrum's commander, 'have you any new developments to report?'

'No, sir; everything's going smoothly. I'm on my way with Captain Brown to rendezvous with the President and escort him to the Spectrum Maximum Security Building. Estimate rendezvous in . . .' there was a brief pause as Scarlet consulted the dashboard computer . . . 'twenty-five minutes.'

'Good,' replied Colonel White. 'Captain Brown, you will take charge of the escort operation. Captain Scarlet, after the rendezvous has been effected, return here to Cloudbase.'

'Yes, sir.' The radio clicked off and the cap microphones flipped back into normal position. Scarlet turned to his comrade. 'Congratulations, Brown,' he said. 'This will be your first big assignment. I wish you luck.'

'Thanks,' said Captain Brown. He was smiling, but there was no disguising the fact that he felt worried. After a moment he added: 'Do you think the

President's life really is in danger?'

'Possibly,' said Captain Scarlet. 'Judging from the report of the Martian expedition, the Mysterons certainly have the power to carry out their threat.'

'If only we were fighting something we understood – something tangible, an enemy we could get to grips with.'

Captain Scarlet nodded. 'I know what you mean. We can only hear the Mysterons on our radios, but I've got a feeling they're with us all the time.'

Even as Captain Scarlet was speaking, a narrow beam of blue light shone out of the sky. The two men in the car failed to notice it strike one of the tyres. There was a flash of searing heat, then a bang as the tyre burst. The car swerved. Scarlet spun the wheel, desperately trying to regain control, but he could see the car was about to go off the side of the road. It was a ten-metre drop to the bottom of a gully.

Scarlet tried the door. Locked! He slammed his hand down on the emergency impact button. It should have inflated air bags to cushion the shock of the crash, but instead there was just a crackle of burned-out wiring from under the dashboard.

'The Mysterons—' Scarlet gasped as the car went over the edge.

Those were his last words. Then the car exploded into flames.

## SMOKING CAN BE FATAL

Colonel White was speaking. Captain Scarlet looked dazed, but he stood to attention as he listened to his commander's words: 'May I congratulate you on your escape, Captain Scarlet. You're a very lucky man – and Captain Brown too. If you hadn't been thrown clear before the car crashed, there would be no way you could have survived.'

Captain Scarlet gazed back without expression. 'Thank you, sir.'

Colonel White nodded. 'All right, let me have your report.'

'The rendezvous went ahead as

planned once we'd radioed for another car,' replied Captain Scarlet. 'The streets of New York have been cleared for two blocks on either side of the President's route and guards have been placed on the roof of all strategic buildings.'

Colonel White leaned forward and flicked open a radio link. 'Captain Brown,' he said, 'three Angels should now be overflying your motorcade.'

Captain Brown heard the familiar drone of the Angels' jets as they went whooshing overhead. 'Spectrum is green,' he told Colonel White over the radio.

The World President, sitting next to Captain Brown in the armour-plated limousine, was obviously very impressed. He looked out through thick bullet-proof glass at the empty streets. 'Spectrum certainly isn't taking any chances,' he said.

Captain Brown snapped his micro-

phone back up along the peak of his cap, shutting the communication link to Cloudbase. 'No, indeed, Mr President,' he replied. 'This vehicle is built to withstand all but a direct hit from any conventional warhead. We have armed guards on the rooftops up there, helicopters and the Angels overflying our position. No enemy could get within half a mile of you.'

'I'm impressed by all these precautions, Captain. All the same, I'll be happier when we reach our destination. These Mysterons . . . we're dealing with an enemy who doesn't follow the usual rules of engagement.'

Captain Brown gave him an odd look as he said this, but the President failed to notice. His attention was focused on the building dead ahead: a Spectrum Maximum Security centre. Its walls were of reinforced concrete nearly two metres thick. The limousine glided across an armoured concourse and the two men climbed out on to a moving walkway.

Just ahead of them, a number of armed security agents were facing a security arch. The walkway paused as the President passed under the arch and a green light came on.

'Just an electronic check, Mr President,' said Captain Brown as he came up behind. 'You're obviously carrying no weapons.'

As Captain Brown himself passed through the arch, however, a red light showed and a shrill klaxon began to sound. The security agents were instantly alert, training their guns on Captain Brown. They were trained to take no chances.

Captain Brown just smiled. 'It's OK, don't panic,' he said. Reaching into his jacket, he pulled out a metal cigarette case and tossed it into a nearby litter

bin. 'I'd been meaning to give up smoking anyway.'

The President gave a sigh of relief. The Mysteron threat had clearly left him on edge. 'For a moment there you had me worried, Captain Brown,' he said as the two stepped into an elevator.

A row of lights checked off the floors as they descended deep under the ground. Finally the elevator drifted to a halt and the doors opened to reveal a sumptuously furnished luxury apartment. They stepped out on to a deep-pile carpet.

'As bunkers go, it looks a lot more comfortable than I expected,' murmured the President, looking around approvingly.

Captain Brown nodded. 'It's the Presidential Suite, sir.'

The President laughed. 'It'll be our home for the next few weeks. I hope you play a good game of chess.'

'I play a very good game.' Again Captain Brown gave him that intent look, and again the President did not notice. He was too busy admiring the fine walnut-wood desk that Spectrum had provided for him.

As he sat down at the desk, the President spotted a lens poking from the wall between two paintings. 'What's that?' he asked, turning to Captain Brown. 'A camera?'

The strange look stayed in the Spectrum officer's eyes as he answered: 'Our every move is being watched.'

Was it only the President's imagination, or had an odd sinister tone crept into Captain Brown's voice? He sounded like an actor who couldn't be bothered to keep up his part any longer. The President decided it was just his nerves playing tricks on him. 'I see I've nothing to fear while I'm in the hands of Spectrum.' He paused. Captain Brown said nothing. Uncomfortable in the silence, the President went on: 'I was saying, Captain Brown . . . I have no need to worry as long as your organization is looking after me.'

Brown stayed immobile like a wax dummy, staring at the President as though looking right through him.

'Captain Brown, are you all right—?' The President's question went unanswered, but he now noticed that the Spectrum agent's jacket was starting to smoulder. There was the distinctive smell of Maltex fumes – a deadly plastic explosive. Captain Brown had ignited the fuse of a bomb!

In the nick of time, the President hit the red emergency button on the arm of his chair. Immediately clamps sprang out from the back of the chair and locked him safely in place and the chair went hurtling backwards. A concealed tunnel opened in the wall, and as the President was whisked through

this a steel door dropped in front of him, sealing the room.

The chair went whizzing at break-neck speed along an underground tunnel. The President had just time to think that it was rather like a bizarre fairground ride, then he heard a muffled explosion reverberate through the ground. It caused cracks to appear in the tunnel roof and trickles of rock dust fell all around him, but the tunnel held.

The President reached another chamber, where Spectrum agents helped him out of the chair. He looked along the tunnel. 'Captain Brown must have been a traitor,' he gasped. 'A kamikaze assassin! His clothing was packed with Maltex. You've got to warn the people in the Security Building – evacuate them.'

One of the men looked up from a video screen. He wore a shocked expression as he announced, 'It's too late, Mr President. The explosion blew out the building's foundations. It's been completely destroyed.'

The President leaned over the console and stared at the screen. The man was right. Where the Spectrum building had stood was now a heap of rubble engulfed in flames. The President steadied himself, feeling faint. He was sorry for the people who had been killed, and ashamed at the selfish thought that he couldn't help from running through his mind:

*Another second and I'd have been buried under that!*

Later at Cloudbase, the President met with Colonel White to review video tapes of the incident. The cameras had caught everything up until the moment when Captain Brown's concealed packet of Maltex ignited. As the screen went black, Colonel White turned away with a grim look. 'It appears that the bomb that Captain Brown was carrying on his person may have been the trigger for a much larger device planted elsewhere in the building,' he muttered. 'At any rate, the destruction was total. You only just got out in time, Mr President.'

'I know.' The President shook his head, still dazed by the narrowness of his escape. 'So you're saying that Brown was a Mysteron spy?'

'Captain Brown was one of my finest men. That's one of the few things I can be sure of at this time. Since the expedition to Mars there have been a number of peculiar incidents. Captain Black, who led that expedition, was also a trusted agent – but he disappeared after his return to Earth. He never reported for debriefing, and now cannot be found.'

The President sighed. 'And what's our next move?'

'We must show the Mysterons that we will not give in to their terrorism. Captain Scarlet will be escorting you to a Maximum Security Building in London.' He turned as Captain Scarlet entered the room. 'Captain, the life of the World President is in your hands. The Angels will accompany you, but be on your guard. I hardly need remind you that we are dealing with forces we do not comprehend. Anything can happen.'

Scarlet nodded. 'Indeed it can, sir.' He snapped a smart salute and led the President off to the launch deck.

Colonel White watched their takeoff from the window of the bridge. It never failed to stir him when he saw jets roaring across the runway and launching off into the sky. Here, permanently hovering miles above the

ground, was the ideal place for Spectrum's headquarters. In Cloudbase the very ethos of Spectrum was symbolized: the watchful guardian angels of the planet Earth.

A bleep signalled an incoming radio message. Lieutenant Green flicked a switch and said: 'Spectrum control.'

'This is Spectrum New York reporting,' said a voice over the radio. 'We've examined the scene of the car crash. Human remains have been definitely identified by dental records as Captain Brown. Another body was found, also badly charred. Examination is pending on that one.'

Green turned to the Colonel. 'What does it mean, sir?'

Colonel White rubbed his jaw thoughtfully. 'It means the Captain Brown who tried to blow up the

President was an impostor. Something must have happened after the crash — something we don't understand.'

'But Captain Scarlet was in that crash.'

'Captain Scarlet! Whatever happened to Brown could have happened to him, too. Lieutenant Green, contact Destiny Angel and tell her to escort Captain Scarlet back to the carrier immediately. The President is in grave danger.'

## SCARLET SHOWS HIS TRUE COLOURS

Captain Scarlet's plane was just crossing the English Channel as a call came through from the Angel flight escorting them: 'Captain Scarlet, you are to return to Cloudbase at once. Do you read me?'

Captain Scarlet said nothing. The President looked at him and felt a sudden stab of dismay. Scarlet's expression reminded him of what had happened with Captain Brown. 'Aren't you going to answer her?' he asked. But he already knew the answer.

The radio blared again and Destiny's

voice broke through the static: 'Captain Scarlet, this is your final warning. Alter course for Cloudbase, or we shall force you to land.'

Thirty seconds went by. Captain Scarlet did not acknowledge the message. He kept the plane on a level course, gazing into the sky ahead as though in a trance. He did not even bat an eyelid as Destiny Angel sent a missile shooting past the plane.

The President was frantic by now. 'Return to base, Scarlet!' he snapped, but his order was ignored. In desperation he made a grab for the radio and yelled into it: 'Spectrum, this is the President. Captain Scarlet is under alien contr— *unh!*'

Captain Scarlet flung out his fist like a disturbed sleepwalker and the President slumped stunned in his seat. As the Angels came in for another pass, Scarlet pressed the eject button. The cockpit cover snapped open and rockets blasted the two men clear.

From high above, Destiny Angel watched the plane spiral in a nosedive towards the ground. After a moment she saw the bloom of white that told her Captain Scarlet's parachute had opened. She followed it down so as to be able to report their landing spot. After a few minutes she radioed Cloudbase, saying, 'Captain Scarlet and the President have landed. I can see their parachutes in a field near the road. Scarlet has taken the President at gunpoint to a nearby car, and they are now heading in a northerly direction.'

As soon as he had Destiny's report, Colonel White relayed it to Spectrum's London base. He told them that Captain Scarlet and the President had bailed out ninety miles south-west of London city centre, and ordered the nearest Spectrum Pursuit Vehicle on the road immediately.

'Roger, Cloudbase,' came the reply. 'We will establish a radio link from

Spectrum Pursuit Vehicle A-Six-Nine direct to Destiny Angel so as to co-ordinate tracking of the car. Captain Blue should have the SPV up and running within five minutes.'

As they were speaking, Blue was already pulling up at a quiet service station in Surrey. It was not yet 6:00 AM, and the place was deserted except for a single attendant. Blue leaned out of the window, flashing his security pass. 'Captain Blue of Spectrum. I'm here to pick up SPV A-Six-Nine.'

The attendant wiped his greasy hands on his overalls and scrutinized the pass. 'Right you are,' he said. 'It's in that lorry over there. I'll have it ready in a jiffy.'

At the touch of a button, the sides of

the lorry dropped down, revealing the
sleek armoured form of a Spectrum
Pursuit Vehicle. Blue climbed inside
and settled himself in the unusual
driving position – facing backwards.
This had been found to be safer if
the SPV crashed at high speed. A TV
screen lit up in front of him, showing
the view seen by the vehicle's forward-
facing camera. Blue took a moment
to familiarize himself with the controls. It took a while to get used to
facing backwards and driving by TV
monitor, since momentum worked in
the opposite direction whenever you
accelerated or turned a corner, but
Blue had put in many hours of
practice with SPVs and had expert
ratings. As he gunned the motor to
life and steered the SPV out on to the
main road, he was confident he would
soon catch up with the renegade
Scarlet. No car could match an SPV
for speed or road handling.

Destiny called him on the radio.

'Captain Blue, we're tracking the car from the air. It is a white saloon, registration number CR2XOO. It's just turning on to the M21 in the direction of London.'

'Destiny Angel, I've joined the M21. I should be seeing Captain Scarlet's car within four minutes.'

Destiny switched radio channels to put her in contact with the other Angels. 'Rhapsody, there are only two routes Captain Scarlet's car can now take. One leads to the city centre, the other terminates at the Car-Vu skypark. Peel off and destroy the viaduct on the London road. Let's force Scarlet to take the high road.'

Rhapsody gave the famous Spectrum call-sign indicating she understood: 'S.I.G.' Dipping her plane low towards the road, she began her attack run. This was exhilarating. There was no denying the fun in blowing up a section of motorway. Even though they were on a serious mission, these were moments she enjoyed most. Of course, Spectrum would have to pay for repairs later, but this was the kind of bold action that Rhapsody loved. 'It's a good thing it's so early in the morning,' she radioed to Destiny as she released her missile. 'I could never make this shot without blowing up at least one motorist otherwise.'

The viaduct exploded in a billowing of red fire and thick black smoke.

Captain Scarlet's car was only a few hundred metres off when he saw the missile hit. He reacted at once to the forced change of plan, swerving to take the road that led to the Car-Vu skypark.

The road began to slope upwards, and dead ahead they could now see the tower of the skypark. A spiral ramp wound up to the top of a tower five times higher than any multi-storey carpark, where a concrete platform gave a breathtaking view of London and the surrounding countryside. During the day the Car-Vu was normally crowded with sightseers. At this early hour it was deserted. Captain Scarlet accelerated, crashing through the ticket barrier at the bottom of the ramp.

The President had come round from the blow he had taken earlier. He wiped a smear of blood off the corner of his mouth. 'You must be crazy, Scarlet – or you've been brainwashed!'

he said. 'Once we get to the top of the Car-Vu, there's nowhere else to go. Give up now before it's too late.'

There was no reply. Scarlet's eyes gleamed with an eerie alien light now. He was completely in the power of the Mysterons.

# SPECTRUM GETS AN EDGE

Blue reached the Car-Vu. It felt odd to be veering up the ramp and yet to feel himself pushed in the opposite direction by centrifugal force. Opening a security channel on the radio, he put through an all-purpose request for assistance: 'Calling Spectrum helicopter patrols in the vicinity of the Car-Vu skypark. Request you divert nearest patrol to provide back-up.'

'This is Helicopter A-Four-Two,' came a voice back over the radio. 'I am heading towards the Car-Vu, and will rendezvous in one minute.'

With a screeching of tyres and the protesting whine of brakes, Scarlet sped up the ramp. His lighter car gave him the advantage he needed to stay ahead of the SPV. The Angels flew over to observe, but it seemed they were powerless to intervene. They could not use their missiles without blowing up the man they were trying to save. Destiny saw the car reach the top of the skypark and screech to a halt. Scarlet dragged the President out and over to the edge. *Oh, no*, she thought, *he's going to push him off* . . .

But in fact Scarlet's orders were to capture the World President alive. He forced him to climb out along a gantry which supported a communications dish on the side of the tower. Seeing them hanging there hundreds of metres up, Destiny thought they looked like tiny fragile specks.

The SPV was at the top now. 'Helicopter A-Four-Two, you know the situation,' said Captain Blue over the radio. 'As soon as you get here, your target is Captain Scarlet. He is to be considered an impostor, and your orders are to shoot to kill. Then winch the President to safety. All this if I don't get there before you.'

Captain Blue got out of the SPV and strapped on a personal jet pack. Its small fuel tanks could keep him airborne for only five minutes. Not long, but it would have to do . . .

The droning beat of rotor blades could be heard as the helicopter came swooping towards the tower. Blue spoke into his cap microphone: 'Helicopter A-Four-Two, Scarlet is located on the western corner of the skypark. I'll hang back while you go in; you have better cover than I do.' Blue paused, but got no answer other than a buzz of static. He peered at the approaching helicopter. Strange – was it a trick of the light? He couldn't see anyone at the controls. 'A-Four-Two, are you receiving me? Please acknowledge.'

The only reply was a hail of machine-gun fire as the helicopter went thundering overhead. Captain Blue twisted the throttle of his jet pack, soaring out of the way just as red-hot bullets shattered the concrete below where he had been standing. He flipped on his personal radio. 'Destiny Angel,' he said urgently, 'Helicopter A-Four-Two is firing at me, and must now be considered a hostile target.'

Captain Blue was forced across towards the gantry where Scarlet had taken the President. Gunshots rang around his ears. Drawing his own gun, he tried to return fire, but his first bullet ricocheted off the gantry. Behind him he could hear the thudding blades of the helicopter as it came in for another sweep. Another

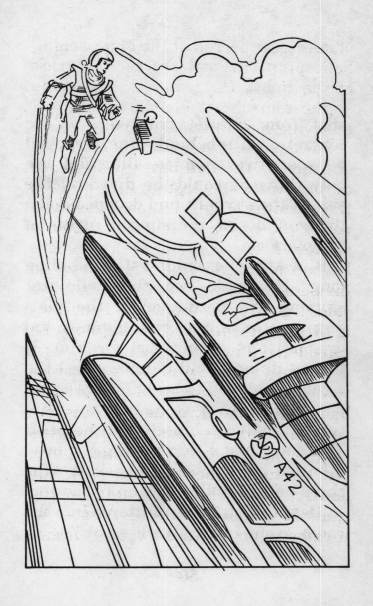

shot from Scarlet cracked into the concrete wall behind him. Trapped between two enemies, Blue did the only thing he could: he dived off the side of the skypark and dropped down to hover beside the support struts of the platform.

Blue knew he couldn't stay in hiding long. He could see the helicopter skirting the perimeter of the platform, appearing like a giant metal dragonfly as it searched for him. It dipped its nose and gunfire raked the structure just off to his left. Blue's eyes widened in shock as he saw now that the helicopter definitely had no pilot. There was just a shimmering rainbow-coloured light inside the cockpit. Was there no end to the Mysterons' power?

'Destiny Angel,' he muttered into the radio, 'come in for attack – now!'

Blue listened for the scream of jets that told him the Angel was getting closer. Hovering into a better position, the helicopter spat out another hail of gunfire, and this time Blue felt something graze his forehead. He knew it couldn't have been a bullet — those high-speed shells would have split his skull apart. Weaving in mid air, he used one hand to control the jetpack while he dabbed with the other at his head. There was a thin trickle of blood, but nothing serious. Blue realized he must have been hit by a flying splinter of concrete.

The helicopter bore closer. Blue would be dead if he stayed where he was. The roar of the Angel's jets sounded like being in the heart of a lightning-stroke. She must be skimming directly across the top of the skypark.

Blue was counting on the Mysterons overlooking something. Their

light-beams might be able to steer the helicopter, but they couldn't hear the Angel's jets. He turned the jet pack on full. The sudden jolt of the thrusters sent him flying up above the rim of the skypark. The copter followed, tilting its nose to get Blue in its sights.

Blue turned his head. The Angel was only a hundred metres off and flying straight towards the helicopter. He turned off the jets and fell, letting his momentum carry him to a rough but safe landing on the skypark platform. As he landed he felt the hot breath of the Angel's jets as she screeched overhead, followed by a massive boom as her missile smashed the Mysteron-controlled helicopter out of the air. Blue crouched and sheltered his head as bits of burning debris showered on to the tarmac around him.

On fire and out of control, the shattered helicopter plummeted out of the sky. There was a low whine as its rotors wound down, followed by a boom as it slammed into the support strut of the tower and dropped blazing towards the ground. Weakened by the impact, the skypark began to collapse.

Blue fired up his jet pack and went whizzing towards the gantry where Scarlet was holding the President. There wasn't much time left. The whole structure gave a sickening lurch. One of the other gantries broke away, and Blue could see the girders twisting under the strain. 'Give it up, Captain,' he said. 'You don't stand a chance. The whole skypark's going to fall. Throw down your gun and I'll fly over to pick you both up.'

'You heard him, Scarlet,' urged the President. 'Do what he says.'

Scarlet hardly seemed to hear them. The look in his eyes was as though he had been hypnotized. Raising his pistol, he pumped three shots at Blue. Luckily the skypark tower shifted further as he fired, and the bullets went wide.

'OK, Captain Scarlet,' said Blue. 'It's you or me.' He had the advantage now, since his jet pack kept him stable enough for a straight shot. His first bullet rebounded off the gantry with a sharp ringing sound, but the second caught Scarlet in the shoulder. The renegade captain gave a brief cry and then toppled off the gantry, tumbling helplessly down towards the ground far below.

Blue felt an instant of nausea. Captain Scarlet had been his friend as well as his colleague, and now the Mysterons had forced him to kill him. But there was no time to brood on that now. Steering the jet pack, he swept in towards the President and caught

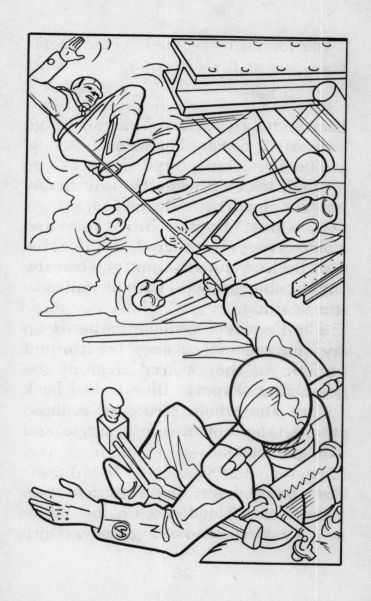

him under the arms. 'You can let go now, Mr President,' he said.

The President stared down at the ground, his eyes wide. He was visibly shaken. 'I can't . . .' he gasped.

'You must!' Captain Blue's voice had the firm tone of command. 'Sir, if you're still holding on to the gantry when the tower collapses, we'll both be pulled to our death.'

The President nodded, gathered up his courage with a deep breath, and let go. As they soared clear of the crumbling skypark, Blue looked back to see the whole structure collapse into a tangle of broken concrete and mangled steel.

Two hours later, the President was back aboard Cloudbase. Colonel White was shaking his head glumly. 'Once

again we managed to foil the Mysterons,' he said. 'But there seems to
be no end to their devilish tricks. They
can keep trying any time they like —
they're making the rules, and they
suffer no losses.' He turned to the
assembled Spectrum agents. 'Gentle-
men, I'm going to be honest with
you. Unless Spectrum gets an edge,
we're destined to lose this war.'

'What about the autopsy on Captain
Scarlet's body, sir?' Lieutenant Green
reminded him. 'You said it might give
us some clues to Mysteron science.'

'That's right.' The colonel spoke into
the intercom: 'Dr Fawn, do you have
that autopsy report on Captain Scarlet
yet?'

'Um . . . no, Colonel,' came the reply.
'There's a problem.'

'What kind of problem?' demanded
White.

'Captain Scarlet is not dead.'

Colonel White and the President
rushed straight to the sick bay. 'Now,

what is all this, Doctor?' said White. 'Scarlet was shot, then fell hundreds of feet to the ground. How can he not be dead?'

Dr Fawn led them through into the next room, where a bandaged Captain Scarlet lay surrounded by instruments. 'When the Spectrum ambulance found him, every bone in his body was shattered and there were no vital signs,' the doctor explained. 'As they put him on to a stretcher, one of the orderlies detected a faint pulse. By the time they were approaching central London, brain activity was restored and his heartbeat was stable. I had him flown here to Cloudbase. I know it's incredible, but by the time he got here all bones had reknit and the worst injuries I could find were bruises. Even they've mostly gone by now.'

Captain Scarlet opened his eyes. 'Colonel . . . Mr President . . .' he said, obviously bewildered. He looked around at the nurses, then sat up.

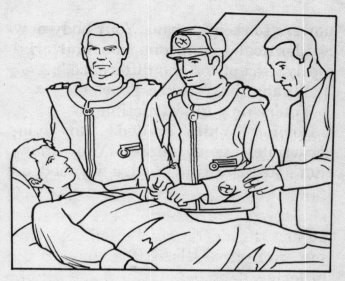

'What am I doing here? The car went out of control . . .'

'So did you!' said Colonel White. 'I'm glad to say you're free of the Mysteron influence now, though.'

Captain Scarlet was staring at the faint bruises on his hands. 'How did I survive the crash?' he asked.

'In a way, you didn't,' said Dr Fawn. 'The charred body we found in the wreck was yours, but it seems the Mysterons used their matter-to-energy powers to recreate you. Your body now is identical to the one you had originally, except for one difference.'

'What's that?' asked Scarlet.

'You're now indestructible.'

Colonel White smiled. 'An indestructible agent, hmm? You know, that's just the kind of edge we needed.'

THE END

# CAPTAIN SCARLET AND THE MYSTERONS

## NOOSE OF ICE

### Dave Morris

*This is Captain Black relayinq instructions from the Mysterons. The mining complex must be destroyed!*

Earth is under attack from the Mysterons. Leading the fight against the Mysterons is one man fate has made indestructible: Captain Scarlet.

Captain Scarlet sets off to the North Pole when a natural source of tritonium – a rare alloy vital to the progress of Earth's space programme – is discovered there. But the Mysterons have attacked, cutting the main power line to the mine. As the sea freezes and a deadly ring of ice slowly closes in, Captain Scarlet faces a race against time to save the complex from total destruction . . .

An explosive and action-packed adventure based on an episode from the sensational TV series.

0 552 527874

# CAPTAIN SCARLET AND THE MYSTERONS

## LUNARVILLE 7

### Dave Morris

*This is the lunar controller. I have been able to contact the Mysterons . . .*

Earth is under attack from the Mysterons. Leading the fight against the Mysterons is one man fate has made indestructible: Captain Scarlet.

When the lunar controller announces that he is negotiating a peace treaty between the Moon and the Mysterons, Captain Scarlet blasts off to the Moon to investigate – and discovers a secret Mysteron base under construction. Trapped in the lunar complex, Scarlet must escape. If he fails, the Mysterons will take control of the Moon . . .

An explosive and action-packed adventure based on an episode from the sensational TV series.

0 552 527882

# This is the voice of the Mysterons...

After a landing on Mars by a Spectrum exploration vehicle, Earth is under attack from the Mysterons.

As Captain Scarlet and the other Spectrum agents prepare to defend the Earth against this terrible threat, they know that anything could happen. For the Mysterons have powers beyond the understanding of man – and they are determined to destroy all life on Earth! Captain Black becomes the Mysterons' pawn, and Captain Scarlet takes on a vital job, escorting the World President on a dangerous journey. But can Scarlet resist the deadly powers of the Mysterons?

An explosive and action-packed adventure based on the first episode of the sensational TV series.

ISBN 0-552-5278

UK £2.50

9 780552 52786